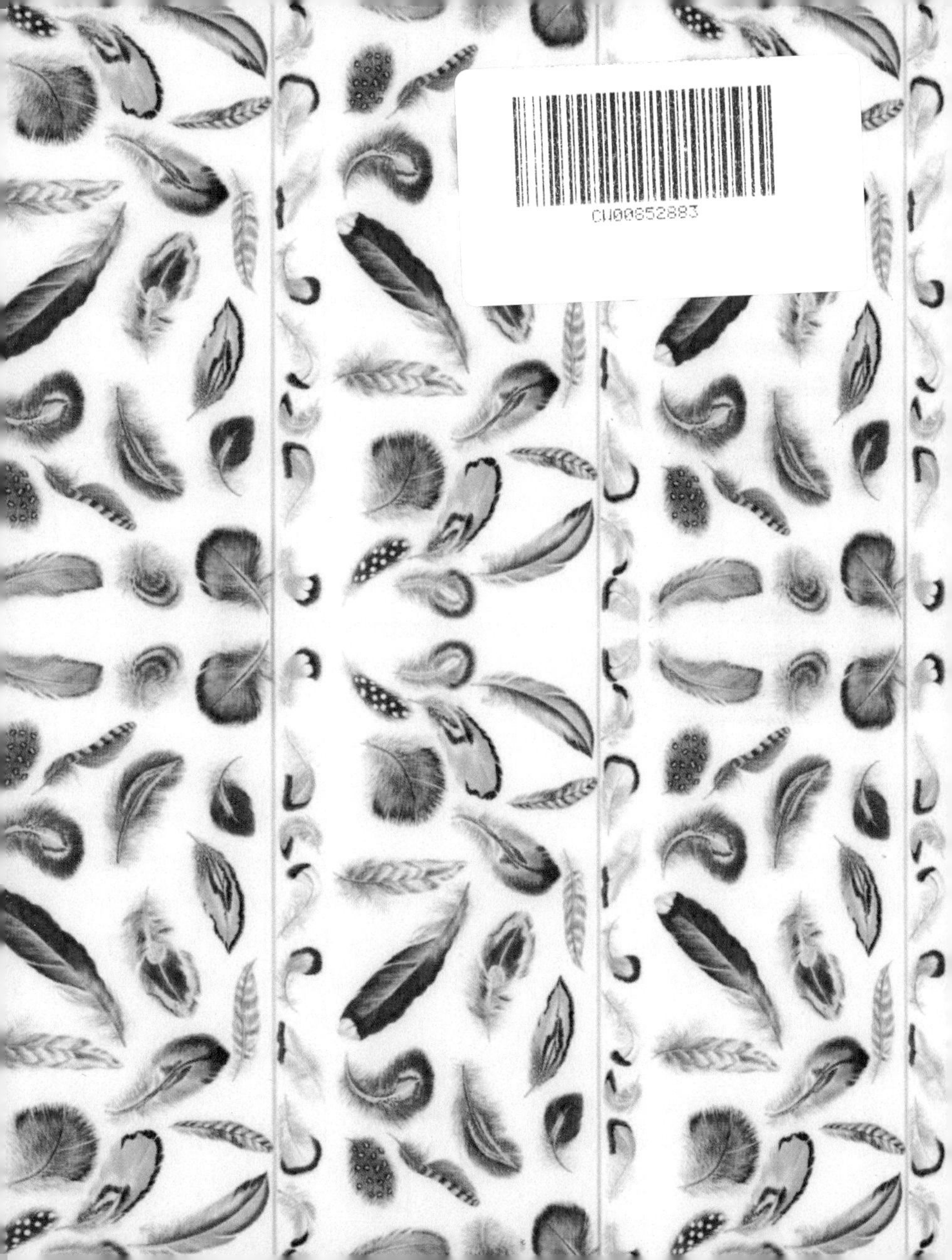
CW00852883

First published in the United Kingdom in 2017 by Jani Tully Chaplin
 ISBN 978-1-5272-0746-2

Enquiries to jani@themanorhousestories.co.uk
www.janitullychaplin.com

Printed and bound in the UK by Cambrian Printers, Aberystwyth
Typesetting and design by JS Typesetting Ltd, Porthcawl, Mid Glamorgan

The Manor House Stories are a series of books for children and the young at heart. They were originally conceived and written nearly thirty years ago while Jani was raising her own two children, Rory and Miranda, at their manor house in the Devonshire countryside.

Foreword by Julian Fellowes

The Manor House Stories create a wonderful and detailed world in miniature full of truth and consequence, like all good stories should, giving us lessons about life but in the most charming way imaginable. No one can accuse the book of soft-soaping the realities of work in a great house; there is plenty of elbow grease required from all the animals and birds employed there, as I should know, but you will find kindness in these pages too, and I suppose I believe that while fate may be challenging for everyone, there is often some kindness in the mix. In my experience anyway. These lovely little tales contain comments and observations that will be very useful to young readers in the years to come, and they will be useful to older readers, too, if I am anything to go by.

The Manor House Stories

Cream & Sugar the Milkmaids The first snow has fallen and the youngsters have fun in the garden. A mysterious visitor arrives in a beautiful sleigh. Erminetine Stoat makes an ice sculpture and is rewarded with a special gift.

Rory Redshank the Footman The Prince's visit causes a stir. Rory has an accident with the red carpet and Delia Duck the Cook bakes heart-shaped biscuits for the Prince on St. Valentine's Day. Rory mislays his precious gold coin.

Sarah Sparrow the Scullery Maid Sarah meets Jeremy Jackdaw the Chimneysweep. Romance blossoms and before long Miss. Nimble-Thimble the Reed Warbler and everyone at the Manor House is planning for a Spring Wedding.

Patience Pigeon the Nanny Easter celebrations at the Manor House, an Easter egg hunt and the exciting arrival of the new baby. Patience has an accident at the pond. Who can save the baby? Rory's gold coin is found in Jailbird Jay's nest.

Miss Miranda Mistlethrush Miranda, the eldest daughter in the family, spends hours in the bath. On her 13th birthday a party is held in the garden with a puppet theatre. Granny and Grandpa McGrouse bring a surprise guest from Australia.

Tilly Titmouse the Parlourmaid Tilly breaks a valuable vase and asks Safari Swallow's help to mend it. Meg Magpie the Gypsy arrives with her caravan and tells Tilly's fortune by looking into a crystal ball; in it she sees Tilly meeting a dark, handsome stranger.

These little stories are loosely themed on the months of the year. There is a circularity to the series, as will be seen when all twelve books are published, although each book stands on its own.

Chesterfield Penguin the Butler The Manor House family make a trip to the seaside. The twins, Arthur and Sebastian, launch their new raft. Blown out to sea they call for help. Sailor Oswald Seagull and Chesterfield Penguin are their only hope.

Radish Robin the Gardener Delia Duck makes strawberry jam. The twins try to help Radish decorate the barn for the Harvest Home. Pieces of Eight the Pirate Parrot is caught with his beak in the jam. A surprise awaits the twins.

Sgt. Simon Squirrel the Quartermaster The Manor House Stores come under attack from the Grey Squirrel Gang. Sgt. Simon calls for assistance from his ex-Army chums, the Red Squirrel Brigade, and Octavius Owl the Schoolmaster.

Ottermere Otter the Water Bailiff The Manor House in danger of flooding. Ottermere Otter enlists the help of Barkus Beaver the Carpenter to divert the river. Wartella Peckster the Hairy Woodpecker conjures up an evil plan for Bonfire Night.

Arthur & Sebastian the Willow Tit Twins The twins prepare for a Bonfire Night party and get a fright in the dark woods. Miranda makes Yum Yum Choc Chips. Wartella Peckster the Witch takes her revenge and the twins learn a lesson.

Lady Davina Dove Christmas has come to the Manor House. Everyone busily prepares for the merrymaking. Stockings are hung and the tree is decorated. The youngsters go carol singing in the village. Father Christmas arrives by moonlight and Lady Davina gets her secret wish.

The January, March and December books have so far been published; first edition copies have sold out, but the author expects to reprint these titles in due course.

Chesterfield Penguin the Butler
All at Sea

The Characters in this story

Miss Miranda Mistlethrush

George the Baby Duckling

Seymour Swansdown the Ferryman

Ottermere Otter the Water Bailiff

Barkus Beaver the Carpenter

Sailor Oswald Seagull

Josefina Hoopoe

Pieces of Eight the Pirate Parrot

Jani Tully Chaplin

with love ♡

This book belongs to
Draw yourself here

TO THE MOORS
TO THE SEA
N
W
E
S
JENNYWREN'S POSTOFFICE
THE VILLAGE
THE MANOR HOUSE
THE DAIRY
THE COACH HOUSE
ERMINETINE'S ICE HOUSE
SGT. SIMON SQUIRREL'S STORES
OTTERMERE OTTER'S HOUSEBOAT
SEYMOUR SWAN
SPITCHWICK DAM
MANOR FARM AND ORCHARD
BARKUS BEAVER

Somewhere deep in the heart of the English countryside, many years ago, stood a fine Manor House. In this house lived a family of birds. Upstairs and downstairs they all played their part in looking after it.

In the gardens, in the village and on the farm, the birds and animals worked together in harmony with nature to preserve the traditions and gentle ways of life that have disappeared long ago.

These stories follow the adventures of the characters in their daily lives, from the lowliest scullery maid through the ranks of the household to the head of the family.

From time to time surprising visitors arrive at the house; from a princess to a pirate, you never know who may appear to cast their magic and mischief over the Manor House ...

The warm airs of summer drifted across the hayfields, wafting gently through the open windows of the Manor House.

Swallows swooped over the lawns like dark paper darts and the songs of skylarks could be heard high above in the cornflower blue skies.

Beyond the garden were high hedgerows filled with red campion, wild honeysuckle and dog roses.

Chesterfield Penguin the Butler was feeling uncomfortably warm as he went about his duties that morning.

He was a penguin after all, and penguins preferred much colder weather as a rule.

The stiff, starched collar of his uniform was rubbing painfully and he could think of nothing nicer than slipping into clear cool water for a swim.

But where to find such refreshing cool water?

“Why of course,” he thought to himself. “At the seaside!”

The family always went to the seaside at least once every summer.

Chesterfield gently reminded Lord Peregrine Falcon as he handed him his morning newspaper, which had been carefully ironed by Rory Redshank the footman.

The papers were ironed to dry out the ink so it would not rub off onto the hands of the reader.

Lady Davina Dove always wore a pair of white cotton gloves to read the paper, just in case the ink marked her white feathers.

"Ah yes, um, of course, um, we must go to the beach," said Lord Peregrine absently, without looking up from his paper. "How I loved the seaside when I was a youngster! It seems only yesterday..."

"I must go down to the sea again, to the lonely sea and the sky, and all I ask is a tall ship and a star to steer her by..." he sighed.

Chesterfield knew Lord Peregrine had drifted into a daydream and would not talk any sense for quite some time.

Nevertheless he thought it was safe to begin planning a trip to the seaside for the following day.

Chesterfield asked Delia Duck the Cook to fill a picnic hamper with enough food for the whole day.

There would be cucumber sandwiches, some hazlenut pies, ginger beer and homemade lemonade for the youngsters, and a bottle of elderflower wine for the grown-ups.

Delia ordered a basketful of last autumn's apples and dried blackberries from Sgt. Simon Squirrel the Quartermaster.

His stores in the hollow tree would just about last until this year's fresh harvest, with a little luck.

Arthur and Sebastian, the twins, were very excited indeed. All day they flitted around the garden singing sea shanties.

Neither of them would come in to bed that evening, even when their nanny, Patience Pigeon, told them they would not be allowed to go on the outing the next day.

“Come in at once, you two!” called Patience from the nursery window.

“Way hay and up she rises, way hay and up she rises, way hay and up she rises, early in the morning!” chortled the twins as they flew in.

SWANSDOWN FERRY

The next morning dawned sunny and clear; the sky would soon be the blue of a jay's wing.

The party made its way down to the river, proudly led by Chesterfield looking his most dignified as he carefully carried the heavy picnic hamper.

Lord Peregrine followed Chesterfield, Lady Davina followed her husband, then came Miranda Mistlethrush.

Arthur and Sebastian flew excitedly along the path to the river surrounded by the Manor House mice.

Patience Pigeon carried George the Baby Duckling in his wicker basket, as he was still too young to walk very far.

Sure enough Seymour Swansdown the Ferryman was waiting for them by the side of the pool, bobbing gracefully on the water.

"All aboard who's coming aboard!" cried Seymour Swansdown impatiently. "Time and tide wait for nobody!"

One by one they climbed onto his back; his feathers were silky soft and his huge wings, folded by his sides, made his passengers feel as if they were travelling on a large white ship.

As soon as the family were comfortably settled, Seymour Swansdown eased away from the bank and drifted off downstream.

The water made a gentle swishing sound as they glided along.

Ottermere Otter the Water Bailiff waved to the family as they passed. He was fishing from his favourite boulder by the edge of the river.

“Have a good trip and take care!” he called in his deep, velvety voice.

A gentle breeze whispered in the willows on the river banks as the water began to flow ever faster towards the sea.

In no time at all they could smell the salty air drifting towards them through the tall reeds on the river bank.

PRIVATE FISHING

At last the reeds opened before them and there was the sea, glittering and sparkling in the sun.

Seymour Swansdown took them to a tiny cove surrounded by sand dunes.

Arthur and Sebastian were so impatient to get onto the beach they almost forgot their manners. Patience had to remind them to let their parents get out first.

As with all well planned picnics, there was a great deal of equipment to unload.

Lord Peregrine grumbled as usual about the amount of baggage, but Lady Davina told him every single thing would be needed.

Chesterfield laid out a rug on the smooth sand and placed the hamper in the middle.

The twins were already making a fine sandcastle near the water's edge; it was surrounded by a moat which they hoped the sea would fill as the tide came in.

Miranda picked seaweed and shells to press into a pretty pattern when she got home.

Chesterfield was getting very hot indeed by the time the picnic had been eaten; his black coat attracted the heat of the sun.

"Who wants to go on a boat?" he asked.

"Me!" shouted the twins together.

The boat was a tiny home-made raft, which Barkus Beaver the Carpenter had built for the twins out of small pieces of wood and some rope made from plaited reeds.

Chesterfield had hidden it on Seymour Swansdown's back beneath the picnic hamper, as a surprise for Arthur and Sebastian.

The twins thought it was wonderful; to them it was their own pirate galleon. It even had a skull and crossbones which Lady Davina had painted on the little flag flying from the top of the mast.

"I want to be Long John Silver!" said Arthur.

"You look more like Short Arthur Tin!" teased Sebastian.

When the twins were on board, Chesterfield waded into the shallow water, pulling the raft behind him.

“Now listen you two,” warned Chesterfield as he let go. “Stay very close to the beach where I can keep my eye on you.”

Chesterfield loved the feeling of the cool sea and swam around happily. He dived under the water, a stream of bubbles trailing behind him.

“Oh bliss!” he thought to himself.

When Chesterfield popped up on the surface again he felt a stiff breeze blowing from the land. He had spent rather too long swimming underwater.

Looking behind him, Chesterfield saw to his horror the little raft scudding far out to sea.

The wind was blowing offshore, which made it very dangerous to be in any small boat; anything afloat would quickly get blown away from the land into deep water.

“Fear not, dear boys,” he called.“ Help is at hand!”

Without a moment's delay Chesterfield plunged underwater, where he could swim fastest.

He looked like a black torpedo as he shot beneath the waves towards the raft.

Little fish scattered out of his way as he burst through their shoals.

"Out of my way!" he squawked, in a rather bubbly voice.

The twins were being rocked back and forth and from side to side by the strong wind and the waves.

They were so frightened!

How they wished they had listened to Chesterfield and stayed in the calm water of the shallows.

The twins shouted for help as the waves splashed over the raft, but their cries were carried further out to sea by the wind.

Nobody on the beach had heard Arthur and Sebastian, nor did they notice that the raft was no longer safely in the cove.

The delicious picnic and the warm sun had made the grown-ups very sleepy; now they were all dozing contentedly on the beach.

Luckily for the twins, Chesterfield had not been the only one to notice the twins getting into difficulty.

Their progress on the raft and had also been spotted by another sharp pair of eyes.

The twins' cries had been heard by a large herring gull perched on a rock.

He wore a smart, navy blue peaked cap and had a small spyglass tucked under his wing.

During the summer months this seagull kept watch over the beach and sea.

The visitors were often getting into trouble and he felt it was his duty to save them.

He flew over to the little raft and, with his sharp yellow beak, he grabbed a rope which was trailing in the water.

He turned the raft slowly into the wind and began pulling it gently towards the shore.

But the wind was so strong that the seagull was having trouble pulling the raft against it. Once he nearly lost the rope altogether, which made the twins screech with fright.

Just at that moment Chesterfield shot up out of the water behind the raft.

Paddling madly with his strong webbed feet, he pushed the raft back into the cove with his beak.

Once the twins were safely ashore again, Chesterfield could relax. Wrapping himself in a towel, he turned to Oswald:

“Thank you so much for your timely assistance,” puffed Chesterfield, very out of breath. He was not quite as fit as he used to be in his younger days.

“To whom do we owe our gratitude?”

“Sailor Oswald Seagull,” answered the friendly stranger.

“I'm the Coastguard around these parts, retired from the Navy many years ago now but I keeps meself busy watching out for folks in trouble on the sea. Landlubbers call me SOS for short”

SS
MANOR HOUSE

"Doesn't that stand for something else too?" interrupted Arthur.

"Save Our Souls!" shouted Sebastian brightly.

On the beach Oswald told them about the rules of the sea and how careful they must be in future.

"You youngsters must always stay within your depth, unless you want to end up being carried out to sea," advised Oswald. "Then you'd probably have to send out a real SOS, even if you did have lifebelts!"

While he talked of his life on the ocean wave, Oswald started to scratch the damp sand into a cone shape, patting it down with his wide webbed feet.

Then he dug out a tunnel from one side and made a narrow chimney in the top until it reached the hollow inside.

He told the twins to find some small twigs, bits of paper and dry leaves, which Oswald pushed deep inside the tunnel.

He struck a match and set fire to the paper.

“What on earth is he doing?” asked Sebastian.

“Goodness only knows”, said Arthur. “But we won't get much warmth from that bonfire!”

Suddenly a little wisp of smoke appeared from the hole on the top of the cone.

“Golly!” shouted the twins together. “It's a volcano!”

"That it be!" laughed Oswald in his best pirate voice. "Just like the ones I seen when I sailed the Seven Seas, me hearties."

“Well shiver me timbers!” said the twins, copying an expression they had read in their favourite pirate stories.

Before saying goodbye Oswald showed the twins an old, green glass bottle with a rolled up piece of paper inside.

“What's this for?” asked Sebastian.

“Arr, 'tis a message in a bottle,” explained Oswald. “In the olden days sailors used to seal their messages inside bottles”.

“They would throw one into the sea to be carried off by wind and tide until it was found by someone who could read their message.”

“But these days we don't want to go throwing bottles into the sea, do we? Think of all that sharp broken glass for folks to tread on!”

“So here's two halves of a coconut shell, some string, a scrap of paper and a piece of charcoal instead. I picked it all up from the tideline just this morning when I was clearing the litter”.

"What shall we do with it all?" the twins asked.

"You can write your message on the paper, roll it up inside the coconut shell and tie the two halves together tightly," said Oswald.

"And if you put your address on the back, you might even get an answer from many miles away!" added Oswald.

The twins set to work right away, carefully writing their message on the piece of paper with the charcoal.

When it was finished and tied up tightly they floated the coconut in the shallows, watching it bob away on the waves until it was far out of sight.

"Here's a little present for you," said Oswald. "To remind you of your adventure at the seaside."

He produced a bottle from his duffle bag, a smaller bottle with something inside.

"Is this a message from someone too?" asked Arthur.

When they looked closely they saw a tiny ship inside the bottle. It had masts and sails, ropes and ladders, in fact every last detail of a sailing ship in miniature.

"How ever did it get inside?" asked Chesterfield, fascinated.

“Well now, the model ship is made with masts that fold down flat.” said Oswald. “And each mast has a long piece of cotton tied to it.”

“Then the boat is pushed carefully through the bottleneck,” he continued.

“Once the boat is safely inside, the masts are pulled upright with the cotton threads. The cotton is cut off and the ship looks as if it got inside the bottle by magic!”

“Thank you so much, Sailor Oswald,” said Sebastian.

“We shall treasure it forever!” exclaimed Arthur.

The twins thanked Chesterfield and Oswald for rescuing them and rushed up the beach to show everyone their wonderful present.

Of course they couldn't wait to chatter about their great adventure too.

They flew past Miranda who was busily arranging her shell collection in a neat pattern; she had been far too busy to notice the twins disappearing out to sea on their raft.

Little George was trying to help Miranda with the arrangement but, as she was very particular, he was only hindering.

“Thank you, George, that’s the very shell I needed!” said Miranda kindly, not wanting to hurt his feelings.

Later that evening, tucked up safely in their bed, Arthur and Sebastian gazed at the ship in a bottle on their bedside table.

They wondered how far their coconut shell would float before it reached land.

Perhaps their message would be found by a fisherman, or some poor sailor shipwrecked on a desert island.

With luck they might even receive a letter telling them where their coconut had been found.

Their dreams that night were of sailing ships and brave captains, of fierce pirates and buried treasure.

Below stairs in his parlour, Chesterfield was sitting in his favourite rocking chair. He was thinking about his wonderful swim in the sea.

He planned to return to the seaside soon, perhaps on his next day off. He would like to see his new friend Oswald again and hear more about his adventures on the high seas.

Growing sleepy, Chesterfield's mind drifted back to his younger days when he too had travelled the world.

Chesterfield had visited many countries before he was a butler; he had fond memories of dear friends in far off lands. Most especially he hoped to see Josefina Hoopoe again one day.

He sang an old sea shantie softly to himself:

Farewell and adieu unto you Spanish ladies
Farewell and adieu to you ladies of Spain
For it's we've received orders for to sail for old England
But we hope we shall see you fair ladies again ...

His head nodded, his eyes closed; soon he was fast asleep.

It had been a very exciting day.

Meanwhile, somewhere far, far away on a deserted shore, the twins' coconut shell had been picked up from the water's edge by a strange and colourful character.

He had a wooden leg, a crutch under one wing, and a fine gold ring in one ear.

It was Pieces-of-Eight, the Pirate Parrot himself!

The shell fell open on the sand as he cut the string with his sharp beak. Unrolling the piece of paper carefully, he read the twins' message.

Pieces-of-Eight gazed out to sea, smiled his most mischievous smile and cackled his greediest cackle, as he wondered how quickly he could reach The Manor House ...

How to Make a Seaweed Print

Gather a selection of wet seaweed and some shells. Place in a plastic bag until you want to begin - the same day is best. This next part is messy! Be sure to wear an apron, like Miranda, then cover a table with newspaper.

Lay small pieces of damp seaweed and shells on the paper in a pattern as you like. Take a soft, craft paintbrush and some ready mixed poster paint in a colour of your choice. As quickly as you can, paint every piece of seaweed carefully, trying to keep it position; the paint must stay wet.

Slide pieces of clean white paper under your seaweed until any paint on the newspaper is covered. Place a piece of white cotton material on top; a clean and ironed portion of a pre-loved sheet or pillowcase is ideal.

Ask someone to help you hold the material as you press down very firmly, sliding your hand slowly from one end to the other to make sure every shell and bit of seaweed leaves an imprint.

Slowly lift off cloth and there is your picture!